THE SHIMMERING STONE

written by Carol Reinsma
pictures by Nathan Cori

S ™
STANDARD
PUBLISHING

The Standard Publishing Company, Cincinnati, Ohio
A division of Standex International Corporation
© 1994 by The Standard Publishing Company
All rights reserved.
Printed in the United States of America
01 00 99 98 97 96 95 94   5 4 3 2 1

Library of Congress Catalog Card Number 93-21504
ISBN 0-7847-0007-9
Cataloging-in-Publication data available

Edited by Diane Stortz
Designed by Coleen Davis

CONTENTS

Moss-covered stones

dotted the mountainside.

But Coney did not play

among the stones.

He was too busy making wishes.

"I wish I had

a bright-colored stone," he said.

"I wish I had a shiny stone."

Just then Mouse ran up to Coney.

"What are you doing?"

asked Mouse.

"I am wishing I could have

a bright, shiny stone," said Coney.

Mouse rubbed the orange

and yellow mossy stones.

"I like these stones," said Mouse.

Coney threw a mossy stone.

"I wish for something fancier,"

he said.

"Emerald, rubies,

and diamonds, too," sang Mouse.

"I wish all of your wishes

will come true."

"I have heard about a place
deep in the dark forest,"
said Coney.
"What kind of place?"
asked Mouse.
"A place of shiny stones,"
said Coney.
"But it belongs
to Hawk."
"Then don't go there,"
said Mouse.
"Hawk is known
for his tricks."

"You can't stop me,"
said Coney.
"Nothing can stop me
from getting my wish."

Coney left the mountainside
and traveled far
into the dark forest.

Under the branch
of an old pine tree,
Coney saw a stone.

10

It was a bright stone,

big and round and shiny.

A hawk in a large hat

and a black coat

sat beside the stone.

"Do you want the stone?"
asked Hawk.

"Oh, yes," said Coney.

"It will cost you
everything you have,"
said Hawk.

Coney emptied

his pockets.

"I want your jacket, too,"

said Hawk.

Coney took off

his velvet jacket.

Hawk gave Coney
the shiny stone.
"Thank you," said Coney.
"Now I have the treasure
of my life."
Coney lifted the stone
up to the light.

But it was not a real stone!

It was plastic.

And Coney knew

that his treasure was worthless.

A foolish person will believe anything.
But a wise person thinks about what he does.
Proverbs 14:15

THE TRAP

The hawk grinned at Coney,

but his eyes were mean.

"Don't you like your treasure?"

he asked.

Coney shook his head.

"I have something better,"
said Hawk.

"It is too late," said Coney.
"I already gave you
everything I had."

"This won't cost you a penny,"
said Hawk.

"Bring your plastic stone
and come with me."

Coney followed Hawk

deeper into the forest.

A hollow tree stump was filled

with bright-colored plastic stones.

"These can all be yours,"

said Hawk.

"But first I want you

to do one thing.

Hold up your stone and smile."

Hawk snapped a picture.

"Perfect," he said.

"Now I can show the world."

With a black pen,

Hawk wrote on the picture:

CONEY FOUND HIS TREASURE

AND SO CAN YOU.

"No," said Coney.

"This is not my treasure."

"But if we say it is," said Hawk,

"others will want it, too.

They will give us

everything they have.

And you can share

my shiny stones."

Coney looked

at the bright and shiny stones.

They looked better

than real stones.

They looked more wonderful

than the moss-covered stones

on the mountainside.

Then Coney remembered.

Mouse had said, "Be careful."

"No," said Coney.

"It is wrong."

He grabbed the picture

and tore it up.

The pieces fell on the ground.

Near the pieces of the picture,

Coney saw a small stone

with bits of moss.

Coney picked up the stone.

Then he ran away

as fast as he could go.

Keep your eyes focused on what is right.
Keep looking straight ahead to what is good.
Proverbs 4:25

23

BEAUTIFUL MARBLES

Coney ran out of the forest.

He could see the mountain.

It seemed to touch the sky.

That is where I belong,

he thought.

I must go home.

But it is sad to go home

without a shiny stone.

Then a blue and gold marble

rolled over Coney's toes.

Coney picked up the marble.

No one was around.

Coney slipped the marble

into his pocket and kept walking.

Another marble, red and silver,

rolled close to Coney.

Coney put this one

into his pocket, too.

The marbles clicked

against each other

inside his pocket.

Coney was almost
up the mountainside
when he saw Chipmunk.
All of Chipmunk's books
were on the ground.
Chipmunk was shaking
his head.

"Have you lost something?"

asked Coney.

"Yes," said Chipmunk.

"All my treasured marbles

seem to have rolled away."

"Too bad," said Coney.

Chipmunk ran off

to search some more.

Coney patted the marbles

in his pocket.

Then Mouse saw Coney.

"Emeralds, rubies,

and diamonds, too," sang Mouse.

"Have all of your wishes

come true?"

Coney showed Mouse the marbles.

"What beautiful colors!"

said Mouse.

"You can put those

in a special place

to look at every day."

Suddenly Chipmunk
came running back again.
Coney hid the marbles
in his pocket.
"I will give Chipmunk
the moss stone I found,"
he said.

Coney gave the moss stone
to Chipmunk.

"Thank you," said Chipmunk.
"This is lovely. I will enjoy it
because you gave it to me
when I felt sad."

"Why are you sad?"
asked Mouse.

"I know why Chipmunk is sad,"

said Coney.

Coney put his hand

into his pocket.

He brought out the marbles.

"I believe these

are yours, Chipmunk," he said.

Chipmunk clapped his hands

when he saw the marbles.

"I thought keeping your marbles
would bring me joy,"
said Coney.
"But now I know I can't be happy
keeping something
that isn't mine."

Coney thought about

all the mossy stones

on the mountainside.

Up he ran.

I will find joy

in what I have,

he thought.

Wisdom will help you to be a good person.
It will help you do what is right.
Proverbs 2:20

POLISHED TO PLEASE

The wind rippled
through the air.
Coney sat
on a furry moss stone.
"I wish — " he said.
"I wish I knew
what would make me
happy every day."

38

Then Coney thought
about Mouse and Chipmunk.
He found paper, a pencil,
two envelopes,
and two stamps.
Coney wrote a letter to Mouse
and a letter to Chipmunk.

The letters said,

Please come visit me

on Tuesday at ten o'clock.

You are a part of making

my wishes come true.

Your friend, Coney

Coney mailed the letters.

At ten o'clock on Tuesday,

Mouse and Chipmunk came.

"Emeralds, rubies,

and diamonds, too," sang Mouse.

"Have all of your wishes

come true?"

"Yes," said Coney.

"Now I can be happy every day.

Wisdom, truth, and kindness

are the emeralds, rubies,

and diamonds of happy days."

"Nothing else?" asked Mouse.

"Wisdom, truth, and kindness

are more than enough,"

said Coney.

At lunchtime,

Mouse, Chipmunk, and Coney

ate barley soup

and grass-seed muffins

on a large, flat, mossy stone.

After lunch they giggled
and sang songs.

They danced
and jumped
on the stone.

When it was time

for his friends to leave,

Coney said,

"I wish you would

come back soon."

"I will come back tomorrow,"

said Mouse.

"Me, too," said Chipmunk.

After Mouse and Chipmunk left,
Coney saw that all the moss
had been rubbed off
the large, flat stone.

The dancing of his friends
had polished it.
Now it shimmered and shone.

"Emeralds, rubies,
and diamonds, too!" cried Coney.
"Wisdom, truth, and kindness
have brought me *more*
than happiness."
He ran down the hill
to tell his friends.

Wisdom is pleasing to you.
If you find it, you have hope for the future.
Your wishes will come true.
Proverbs 24:14